YEARBOOK

Based on the Disney Channel Original Movie

TIME INC. BOOKS

PUBLISHER Margot Schupf
ASSOCIATE PUBLISHER Allison Devlin
VICE PRESIDENT, FINANCE Terri Lombardi
EXECUTIVE DIRECTOR, MARKETING SERVICES Carol Pittard
EXECUTIVE DIRECTOR, BUSINESS DEVELOPMENT Suzanne Albert
EXECUTIVE PUBLISHING DIRECTOR Megan Pearlman
ASSOCIATE DIRECTOR OF PUBLICITY Courtney Greenhalgh
ASSISTANT GENERAL COUNSEL Andrew Goldberg
ASSISTANT DIRECTOR, SPECIAL SALES Ilene Schreider
ASSISTANT DIRECTOR, PRODUCTION Susan Chodakiewicz
SENIOR MANAGER, SALES MARKETING Danielle Costa
SENIOR MANAGER, CHILDREN'S CATEGORY MARKETING Amanda Lipnick
SENIOR MANAGER, BUSINESS DEVELOPMENT • PARTNERSHIPS Nina Fleishman Reed
MANAGER, BUSINESS DEVELOPMENT • PARTNERSHIPS Stephanie Braga
ASSOCIATE PREPRESS MANAGER Alex Voznesenskiy
ASSISTANT PROJECT MANAGER Hillary Leary

EDITORIAL DIRECTOR Stephen Koepp
ART DIRECTOR Gary Stewart
ART DIRECTOR, CHILDREN'S BOOKS Georgia Morrissey
EDITORIAL OPERATIONS DIRECTOR Jamie Roth Major
SENIOR EDITOR Alyssa Smith
ASSISTANT ART DIRECTOR Anne-Michelle Gallero
COPY CHIEF Rina Bander
ASSISTANT MANAGING EDITOR Gina Scauzillo
EDITORIAL ASSISTANT Courtney Mifsud

SPECIAL THANKS: Chelsea Alon, Allyson Angle, Curt Baker, Katherine Barnet,
Brad Beatson, Jeremy Biloon, Ian Chin, Rose Cirrincione, Pat Datta, Nicole Fisher, Alison Foster,
Joan L. Garrison, Erika Hawxhurst, Kristina Jutzi, David Kahn, Jean Kennedy, Amy Mangus,
Melissa Presti, Babette Ross, Dave Rozzelle, Divyam Shrivastava, Larry Wicker, Krista Wong

PRODUCED BY DOWNTOWN BOOKWORKS INC.

PRESIDENT Julie Merberg
EDITORIAL DIRECTOR Sarah Parvis
EDITORIAL ASSISTANT Sara DiSalvo
COVER AND INTERIOR DESIGN Georgia Rucker

Published by Time Inc. Books
1271 Avenue of the Americas, 6th floor • New York, NY 10020

ISBN 10: 1-61893-158-X
ISBN 13: 978-1-61893-158-0
Library of Congress Control Number: 2015935933

We welcome your comments and suggestions about Time Inc. Books
Please write to us at:
Time Inc. Books, Attention: Book Editors, P.O. Box 361095, Des Moines, IA 50336-1095
If you would like to order any of our hardcover Collector's Edition books, please call us at
800-327-6388, Monday through Friday, 7 a.m.-9 p.m. Central Time.

Congratulations on another marvelous year! From welcoming a new batch of students to enjoying nail-biting action on the tourney field and witnessing an unforgettable coronation, there hasn't been a dull moment here at Auradon Prep! It has been a pleasure to watch each and every one of you grow and learn.

—Fairy Godmother, Headmistress

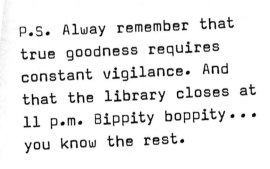

P.S. Alway remember that true goodness requires constant vigilance. And that the library closes at 11 p.m. Bippity boppity... you know the rest.

HIGHLIGHTS
from an Enchanting Year...

Where will we be in 10 years? Check out the career predictions on page 30.

Student profiles start on page 10.

Which subject won the annual favorite class poll? Go to page 32.

What goes on after classes? See pages 34–39.

Tourney rocks! Go, Fighting Knights! Turn to page 36.

Students open up about the things that irk them most. Go to page 40.

Pretty in pink? Dapper in blue? Learn all about Auradon style on pages 46–51.

MAL—
You *are* the baddest of them all! Never forget that, gorgeous.
JAY

Biggest gossip? Most artistic? Find out who took the top honors on page 58.

THE YEAR *in Review*

It's been a big year for Auradon Prep, complete with new students, new classes, and even a new king! Here's a look at just a few of the moments from the past year.

Some HIGHS

A LOVELY DAY FOR CROQUET!

WELCOME, WELCOME!

A NEW REIGN BEGINS!

DANCE YOUR HEART OUT!

PASSING NOTES!

Some LOWS

Note passing, roughhousing,
and garden spats, oh my!

A SCUFFLE ON THE SOUTH LAWN!

GRAFFITI ON THE RISE!

TABLES ARE FOR STUDYING, NOT FOR WRESTLING!

New Year, NEW STUDENTS

Auradon Prep was proud to welcome some new students this year. Mal, Evie, Jay, and Carlos transferred in, straight from the infamous Isle of the Lost. This fearsome foursome made our student body more fashionable and our tourney team more victorious. They also made our school year more . . . um . . . memorable than we could have imagined.

Jay and Carlos make an unforgettable entrance on their first day.

WATCH YOUR STEP!

Mal and Evie survey the scene.

Ben and Audrey are all smiles as they greet the newest members of the Auradon Prep student body.

Ben extends a hand of welcome to the children of the Isle of the Lost.

Meet MAL

FAMOUS PARENT: Maleficent

CLOSEST COHORT: Evie

FAVORITES: Drawing, strawberries, hatching dastardly plots

SECRET WISH: To learn how to swim

NOT-SO-SECRET WISH: To have a different middle name

WOULD NEVER LEAVE THE HOUSE WITHOUT: Her magic spell book, her attitude

Stay good!!
Jane

Move over, Snow White. Mal is making magic in the kitchen!

I LIKE TO MAKE AN ENTRANCE. —Mal

Mal and Jay take a moment between classes.

Purple is this season's hottest color, thanks in part to Mal's stunning wardrobe.

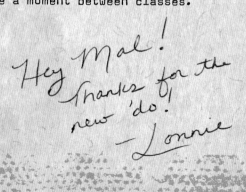

Hey Mal! Thanks for the new 'do! —Lonnie

Introducing EVIE

FAMOUS PARENT: The Evil Queen

CLOSEST COHORT: Mal

FAVORITES: Flirting, apples, sewing

SECRET WISH: To ace chemistry

NOT-SO-SECRET WISH: To live in a giant castle with lots of mirrors and a gorgeous prince who loves her

WOULD NEVER LEAVE THE HOUSE WITHOUT: Her purse, a compact, her special mirror, a killer smile

I DON'T GET MAD, I GET EVIE. –Evie

Evie takes over the keyboard for an after-school study session at Carlos and Jay's room. Popcorn for everyone!

Besties Evie and Mal take Remedial Goodness by storm.

Evie shows off her singular style with her ruffle-necked T-shirt and sparkling heart pendant.

Evie and Doug are unstoppable on the dance floor!

Dearest Mal,
You are like a sister to me. I couldn't have survived life on the Isle without you.
-Evie

P.S.- Remember— when applying blush, always use upward strokes!

Get to Know JAY

FAMOUS PARENT: Jafar

CLOSEST COHORT: Carlos

FAVORITES: Winning, victory pizza

SECRET WISH: For his father to be a very successful businessman and never have to work again

NOT-SO-SECRET WISH: To be on a winning tourney team

WOULD NEVER LEAVE THE HOUSE WITHOUT: His charm

I'VE GOT YOUR BACK. –Jay

Coach Jenkins welcomes Jay to the team.

Go! Fighting Knights!

LADIES' MAN

Jay holds court in the courtyard.

Close-Up on

CARLOS

FAMOUS PARENT: Cruella De Vil

CLOSEST COHORTS: Jay, Dude, Ben

FAVORITES: Giving Dude belly rubs, good friends, video games

SECRET WISH: To run a rescue shelter for abused and abandoned animals (and children)

NOT-SO-SECRET WISH: To never see a fur coat or a bunion ever again

WOULD NEVER LEAVE THE HOUSE WITHOUT: An escape route in mind

YOU AIN'T SEEN NOTHIN' YET. —Carlos

ISLE RULES!
→ CARLOS ✗

Hear Carlos roar on the tourney field!

HEAR ME ROAR! X

Carlos and Jane sure know how to set it off!

No one rocks Isle style like Carlos and Jay!

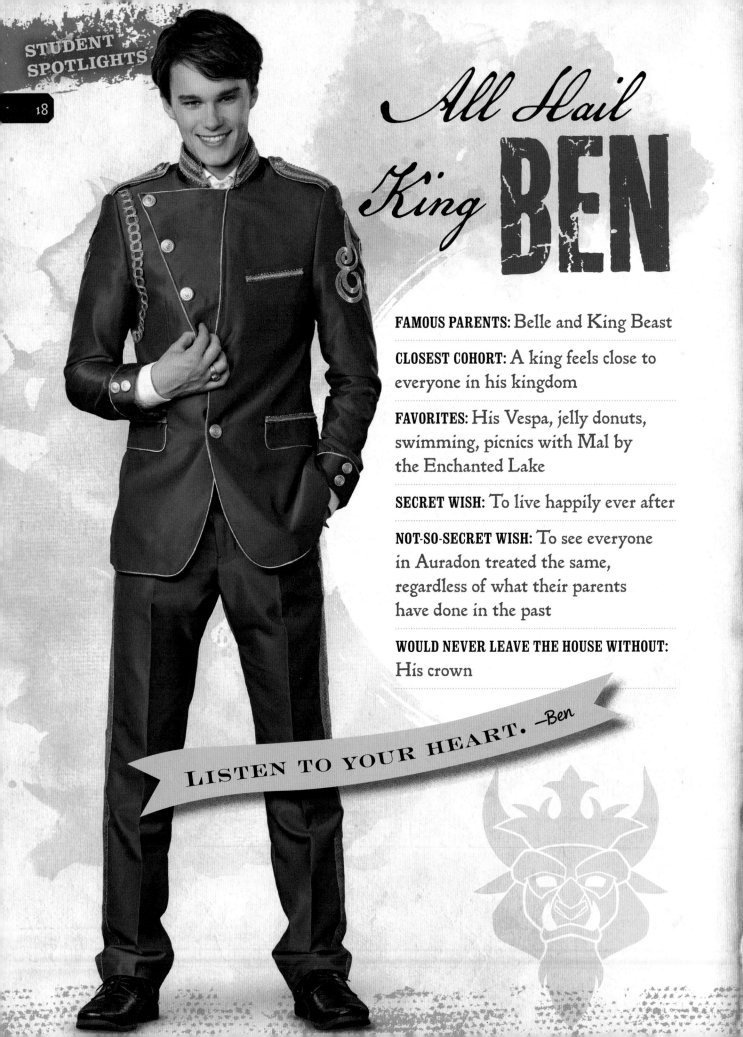

All Hail King BEN

FAMOUS PARENTS: Belle and King Beast

CLOSEST COHORT: A king feels close to everyone in his kingdom

FAVORITES: His Vespa, jelly donuts, swimming, picnics with Mal by the Enchanted Lake

SECRET WISH: To live happily ever after

NOT-SO-SECRET WISH: To see everyone in Auradon treated the same, regardless of what their parents have done in the past

WOULD NEVER LEAVE THE HOUSE WITHOUT: His crown

LISTEN TO YOUR HEART. —Ben

Mal and Ben preside over an unforgettable post-coronation bash.

A picnic with Ben is
a real treat.

Being royal
comes with some
serious perks!

The Audacious AUDREY

FAMOUS PARENTS: Aurora and Prince Phillip

CLOSEST COHORTS: Chad, Lonnie

FAVORITES: Sparkling dresses, being head cheerleader

SECRET WISH: To become queen

NOT-SO-SECRET WISH: To become queen

WOULD NEVER LEAVE THE HOUSE WITHOUT: A flawless outfit and the perfect accessories

SOMETIMES AN EVIL FAIRY IS JUST AN EVIL FAIRY. —Audrey

Ben, Chad, and Audrey are the epitome of Auradon cool.

Audrey and Ben lead the way when the new students arrive from the Isle of the Lost.

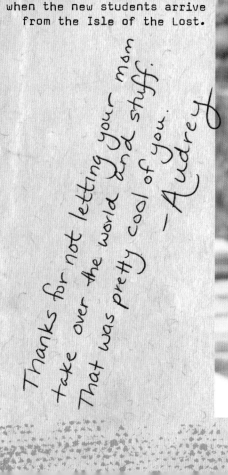

Thanks for not letting your mom take over the world and stuff. That was pretty cool of you. —Audrey

The Unstoppable CHAD Charming

FAMOUS PARENTS: Cinderella and Prince Charming

CLOSEST COHORTS: Audrey, the guys from the tourney team

FAVORITES: Playing tourney, taking selfies

SECRET WISH: To be liked by all the students, even the new kids

NOT-SO-SECRET WISH: To never have to do homework again

WOULD NEVER LEAVE THE HOUSE WITHOUT: Making sure his hair is perfect

NO BIGGIE. MY DAD WILL GET ME ANOTHER ONE. –Chad

Evie and Chad share a moment by the bleachers.

It was a tough day on the tourney grounds for Chad!

Go! Knights! Go!

Win! Win! Win! Win! Win! Win! Win! Win! Win!

Presenting LONNIE!

FAMOUS PARENT: Mulan

CLOSEST COHORT: Audrey

FAVORITES: Long talks with her mom; satin clothes—they're just so shiny!

SECRET WISH: For everyone to be as happy as she is

NOT-SO-SECRET WISH: To be the most fashion-forward girl at Auradon Prep

WOULD NEVER LEAVE THE HOUSE WITHOUT: Her bracelets

CHOCOLATE CHIPS ARE THE MOST IMPORTANT FOOD GROUP. —Lonnie

Remember when Lonnie had bangs? Short hair or long, she always looks incredible!

Audrey, Lonnie, and Ben show off their school spirit on Family Day!

Calling all cookie lovers! Meet us in the kitchen for some late-night munchies!

Here's
DOUG!

FAMOUS PARENT: Dopey

CLOSEST COHORTS: Evie, the guys from the band

FAVORITES: Band practice, studying with Evie

SECRET WISH: To be a rock star

NOT-SO-SECRET WISH: To spend more time with Evie

WOULD NEVER LEAVE THE HOUSE WITHOUT: His glasses

HI HO. –Doug

Lunchtime is the perfect time
for Doug and Evie to dish.

Hi Mal,
It was great getting
to know you and Evie
this year. Especially
Evie. Have a fun summer!
—Doug

Doug's a perfect gentleman,
on the dance floor and off!

A quick chat with Evie
between classes brings
a smile to Doug's face.

Spotlight on JANE

FAMOUS PARENT: Fairy Godmother

FAVORITES: Hanging out with Mal, being the tourney mascot

SECRET WISH: To have a boyfriend who loves her

NOT-SO-SECRET WISH: To only have good hair days forever

WOULD NEVER LEAVE THE HOUSE WITHOUT: A bow

DON'T MIND ME. —Jane

The second-floor girls' bathroom doubles as a hair salon when Jane and Mal get together.

DOUBLE TROUBLE

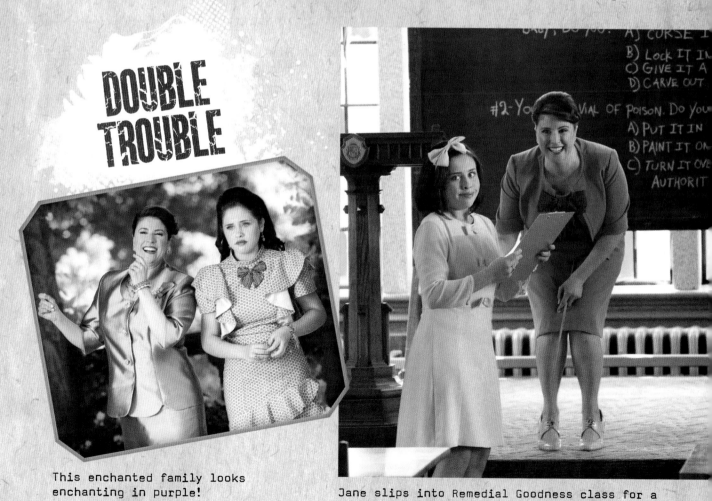

This enchanted family looks enchanting in purple!

Jane slips into Remedial Goodness class for a quick chat with her headmistress...er...mom.

What Will You Be
WHEN YOU GROW UP?

CARLOS:
Dog walker
or app
designer

BEN:
King, founder
of a nonprofit
that helps the
formerly evil

EVIE:
Fashion
designer or
scientist

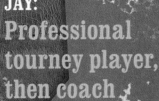

JAY:
Professional
tourney player,
then coach

LONNIE: Host of a talk show about food, family, and culture

AUDREY: CEO of a Royal 500 company

CHAD: Racecar driver, trophy husband

MAL: Artist

Supreme SUBJECTS

Bad Fairies and Dragon Anatomy usually rank high in our annual poll of students' favorite classes. Let's see how this year's courses stack up.

TOP 10 CLASSES

1. Dragon Anatomy
2. Chemistry
3. Bad Fairies
4. Enchanted Forestry
5. Heroism
6. History of Woodsmen and Pirates
7. Mathematics
8. Basic Chivalry
9. Remedial Goodness 101
10. History of Auradon

Fairy Godmother brings her special brand of bippity boppity boo to this year's newest course offering, Remedial Goodness 101.

CARLOS: History of Woodsmen and Pirates. There are very few dogs in those subjects. Not too many parents either.

EVIE: Chemistry. It turns out I'm great at it. Who doesn't like to shine?

DOUG: Chemistry. I sit next to Evie.

What's Your Favorite Class?

MAL: Remedial Goodness 101. The class is a breeze. I just think of what my mom would do, then pick the opposite.

CHAD: Heroism. I mean, it's what I am destined for. Herotown, population: me. Am I right?

JAY: Basic Chivalry, because . . . hello, ladies.

Head cheerleader Audrey helps her squad reach new heights.

After-School ADVENTURES

When classes wind down for the day, the Auradon Prep campus becomes a flurry of activity. The tourney team heads to the field to start running laps and dodging balls in the kill zone. And while the cheerleaders perfect their pyramids and tosses, the marching band warms up.

Chad and Jay go head-to-head in a heated tourney scrimmage.

With the help of his trusty stopwatch, Ben looks to see if Carlos is the next Auradon Prep track star!

Doug takes a break from band practice to meet the young ladies from the Isle of the Lost.

Auradon Tourney RULES!

It's TOURNEY TIME!

The Auradon Prep Fighting Knights are always ready for action on the playing field. Team captain Ben has led the Knights to victory over the Falcons for three years (and counting!). This year's newest players, Jay and Carlos, didn't waste anytime becoming indispensible members of the team.

WATCH OUT! The unstoppable Jay is coming at ya!

TEAM CAPTAIN:
Ben

BIGGEST RIVAL:
Falcons

MOST IMPROVED PLAYER:
Carlos

TEAM LINEUP

Ben	7
Jay	8
Carlos	101
Chad	23
Aziz	11
Brendan	20
Miguel	44
Tyrone	32
Akio	42
William	12

DORM LIFE

When classes are over and activities are done for the day, the students retire to their dorms for studying, sketching, chatting, and, occasionally, plotting world domination. Every dorm on campus has its own distinct style and design.

ROYAL ROOM

King Beast and Belle swing by the royal dorm room to visit their son, Ben.

TOP 5 COOLEST THINGS IN BEN'S ROOM

1. Drum kit

2. Exercise equipment

3. Trophy collection

4. Foosball table

5. Framed concert posters

Jay shares his notes with Carlos.

On artsy evenings chèz Mal and Evie, you'll find Mal drawing, Evie whipping up new fashion-forward creations with her sewing machine, and students dropping by for haircuts and styling tips.

Even Dude makes himself at home in Mal and Evie's room!

Check out some of Mal's drawings!

What's your Biggest PET PEEVE?

CARLOS: Overbearing moms; people who lie to you about sweet, furry creatures; fur coats; bunions

MAL: Sunburns, fake people, perky princesses

JAY: Guys who are mean to women

EVIE: Unruly eyebrows, Komodo dragons, tattletales

AUDREY: Evil fairies, boyfriend stealers

Don't forget me.
— CHAD

CHAD: Not getting my way

JANE: Being ignored, bad hair days

Family Day

One of the year's most special events
brings parents and students together for a day of delicious food,
enchanting games, and tons of fun. On Family Day, parents and siblings
of current students are invited (if they can travel, that is) to campus for
a daylong celebration. It's a tradition—and a treat!

The royal family
poses for a
Family Day photo!

The annual
croquet match
draws an
impressive
crowd.

Hey, Carlos!
Hey, Jay!
Leave some
chocolate-
covered
strawberries
for the rest
of us!

Jay, Carlos, Dude, and Evie live it up on Family Day!

Campus CANDIDS

Auradon Prep is more than your average school. It is home to enchanted statues and unforgettable artwork. A quick walk across campus makes it clear to students and visitors alike that our school is a very special place with a real sense of magic, history, and tradition . . . and goofy students doing ridiculous things.

NEED A NAPKIN?

Um, Carlos. You've got a little something on your face.

Evie shows off her royal curtsy.

LUNCHTIME FAIL!

Looks like someone doesn't like her lunch!

"Hold on for a sec. I really need to take this."

As the spellbinding statue of King Beast morphs from beast to man and back again, some students are awestruck. And others are just plain spooked!

THIS IS WHAT THEY'RE COOKING UP IN THE KITCHEN?

Even four-legged Fighting Knights know how to live it up at Auradon Prep!

Between classes, gal pals can always be found gabbing in the ladies' room.

HURRY UP! OR YOU'LL BE LATE TO CLASS!

Jay says he will crush the competition.

TRENDSETTERS

Every year, students bring their own brand of cool to the halls of Auradon Prep. Last year, pastels and cashmere ruled the school. But this year, an influx of Isle style brought edgier colors and fabrics to our fair shores. See which styles stood out the most.

Doug brings back the bow tie!

It looks like leather gloves are all the rage on the Isle of the Lost. Will they survive the transition to the mainland? Here's hoping.

This is not your grandmother's cape sleeve! Evie has transformed the flowing cape look from "once upon a time" into "hip here and now."

Leather takes center stage in Jay's edgy wardrobe.

Such a fabulous top! ~Jane

Asymmetrical cuts give Mal's distinct style an air of mischief.

Extra zippers take these outfits up a notch on the punk-rock scale.

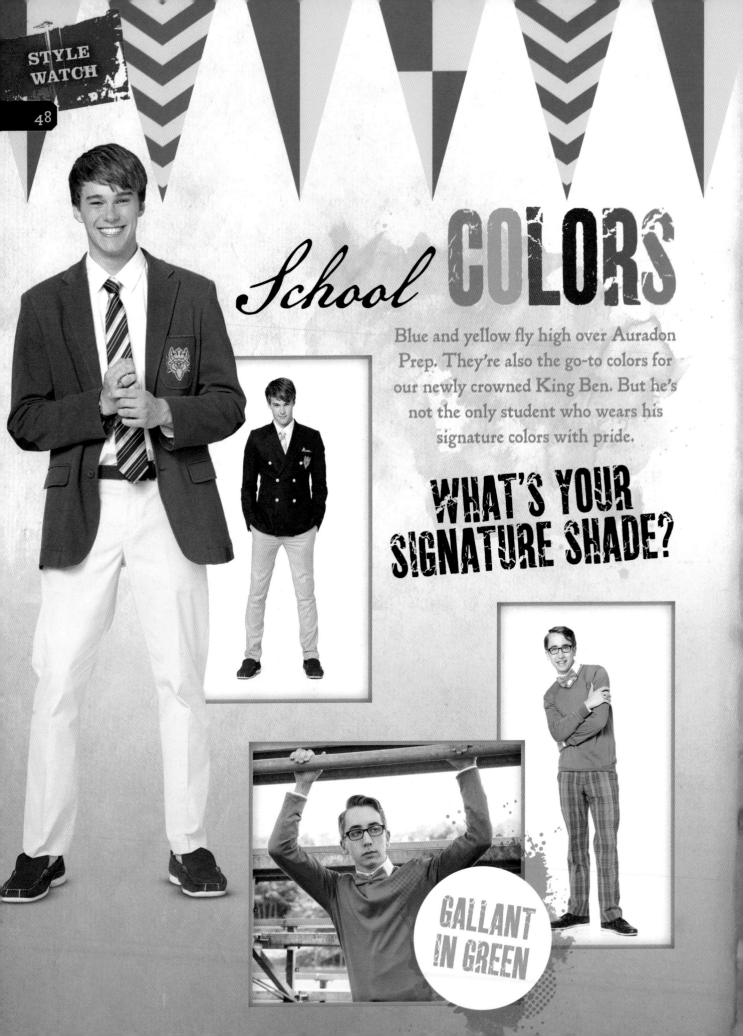

School COLORS

Blue and yellow fly high over Auradon Prep. They're also the go-to colors for our newly crowned King Ben. But he's not the only student who wears his signature colors with pride.

WHAT'S YOUR SIGNATURE SHADE?

GALLANT IN GREEN

Auradon Girls Know How to ACCESSORIZE!

As Snow White always says, "Accessories make the outfit." Here at Auradon Prep, the students never miss a chance to add some bling to a fairy-tale ensemble.
Here are a few standouts.

Lonnie could easily be crowned Queen of the Headband.

Elegant and regal, Evie's tiaras are fit for a princess.

Jane is never fully dressed without a bow (or four or five)!

STYLE SHOWDOWN

Can you match these awesome accessories to the correct fashionista?

1. EVIE OR AUDREY? Match these purses to their stylish owners.

A.

B.

C.

D.

2. LONNIE OR JANE? Can you place these pairs on the correct feet?

A.

B.

C.
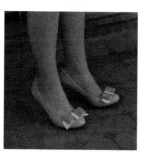

D.

3. MAL OR EVIE? Which pieces of jewelry belong to which stylish student?

A.

B.

C.

D.

Style Showdown Answers:
1. Evie: A, D. Audrey: B, C. 2. Lonnie: A, D. Jane: B, C. 3. Mal: B, D. Evie: A, C.

What Makes You UNIQUE?

Look around at your classmates. Who is most likely to speak at graduation? Who is most likely to toilet paper the King's castle? Who is most likely to invent a usable jetpack to get to tourney practice faster?

Make a prediction! Fill in the blanks for yourself and your friends.

JAY
MOST LIKELY TO... Take two girls to prom!

MAL
MOST LIKELY TO... Be caught stealing candy from a baby ... and giving it back.

BEN
MOST LIKELY TO... RULE MY HEART!

CARLOS
MOST LIKELY TO...
break into the pound and set all of the animals free

DOUG
MOST LIKELY TO...
Invent a really cool ROBOT

EVIE
MOST LIKELY TO...
Be late for class because she's redesigning her outfit

CHAD
MOST LIKELY TO...
Install mirrors in every room of his house

Museum of WONDERS

Sometimes you really need to know about the order of succession in the Great Goblin Kingdom, and other times you might just want to marvel at the glittery jewels in the Crowns of Auradon exhibit. Whether it is for a class or just for fun, we are so lucky to have the Museum of Cultural History just around the corner!

Fairy Godmother's wand is the star attraction of its very own gallery at the Museum of Cultural History.

The entrance atrium of the museum inspires awe in its many visitors.

AURADON

What's Your Go-To Object at the Museum?

Cinderella's glass slipper? King Triton's trident? The magic lamp? Of all the amazing artifacts in the Museum of Cultural History, which one do you think is the coolest?

CARLOS: I like to check out D'Artagnan's sword, hat, and boots. D'Artagnan was one brave guy. I really look up to him. Maybe I should start carrying a sword . . .

MAL: The magic spinning wheel. It looks so boring, but it's kind of spooky that a few pieces of wood could put someone to sleep for 100 years.

EVIE: Whenever I am in the museum (and I can assure you I've only been there during daytime hours), I stop by King Beast's Mystical Rose. It's really beautiful. I'd love for a prince to give me an enchanted rose some day. Well, 12 of them. A whole bouquet of roses would be way better than one measly magical rose. I'm just saying.

JANE: I used to visit my mom's wand a lot. I don't do that anymore.

Gallery of Villains

←

TOP 5 FAVORITE GALLERIES

Once again, the Gallery of Villains came out on top of our annual poll of the students' most-visited rooms in the Museum of Cultural History.

1. Gallery of Villains

2. Gallery of Enchanted Armor

3. Hall of Swords

4. Kingdoms Under the Sea

5. Gallery of Dwarves, Gnomes, and Goblins

Gallery of Heroes

←

FIELD TRIP!

Auradon Prep alumni never forget their trips off campus to Camelot, Charmington, Fortuna, or Belle's Harbor. There's a lot of history to be found all around the United States of Auradon. For a truly relaxing day enveloped in the magic of nature, you don't have to go all the way to Sherwood Forest. You can pop over to our beloved Enchanted Lake.

The Enchanted Lake brings out the Zen in everyone—even Mal!

With a beautiful bridge over a rushing
stream and a lush green forest surrounding
a tranquil lake, a visit to the Enchanted
Lake is the perfect afternoon getaway.

Auradon's #1 couple enjoy a lakeside picnic.

Mal—

My world changed the
moment I met you. I am
the luckiest guy in Auradon.
Love you,
Ben

P.S. Thanks for listening
to your heart!

TOP 5 MOST POPULAR DAY TRIPS

Spooky old Skull Island
knocked the glamorous
court in Cinderellasburg out
of the top spot this year.

1. Skull Island

2. Rocky Point Court in
   Cinderellasburg

3. Grimmsville

4. Neverland

5. Belle's Harbor on the
   Strait of Ursula

Most Athletic

Best Sportsmanship

Biggest Flirt

Most Artistic

Biggest Gossip

A Royal CELEBRATION!

Class projects, exams, all-night study sessions, late-night gossip, weekend trips to Neverland . . . What a whirlwind year! But the event of the year of was, without a doubt, the coronation. People, young and old, came from every corner of the United States of Auradon to see Ben don his royal crown for the very first time.

WE DO NOT BECOME GREAT BY OUR STRENGTH BUT BY OUR COMPASSION! –Ben

Ben and Mal share a quiet moment in the carriage on the way to the cathedral for the coronation.

Ben admits that he was both nervous and excited before he spoke his oath.

A CROWN FIT FOR A KING!

The coronation was an action-packed event, complete with an unforgettable, fire-breathing surprise guest and some shocking revelations. But at the end of the day, what's most important is that Ben spoke the oath that makes him king and that everyone in the realm stayed safe. Phew! All's well that ends well in Auradon!

I solemnly swear to govern the Peoples of Auradon with justice and mercy as long as I reign.

SET IT OFF!

The Coronation Ball was a once-in-a-lifetime event here in Auradon. When the lights went down and the music came up, our students did not disappoint on the dance floor!

Write the book—the story of our lives.

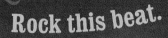

Rock this beat.

Be yourself. Forget the DNA.

Start a chain reaction. Never let it stop!

We got the keys.
The kingdom's ours!